Superfairies

Adventures in
Peaseblossom Woods

by Janey Louise Jones
illustrated by Jennie Poh

SCHOLASTIC INC.

ISBN 978-1-338-28113-2

Text copyright © 2016 by Janey Louise Jones. Illustrations copyright © 2016 by Jennie Poh. All rights reserved. Published by Scholastic Inc., 557 Broadway, New York, NY 10012, by arrangement with Capstone Young Readers, a Capstone Imprint. SCHOLASTIC and associated logos are trademarks and/or registered trademarks of Scholastic Inc.

12 11 10 9 8 7 6 5 4 3 2   18 19 20 21 22 23

Printed in the U.S.A.   40

First Scholastic printing, February 2018

Designed by Alison Thiele and Aruna Rangarajan

For my cousin,
Cathy Brown
— Janey

For my husband Jake,
and our two little fairies
Aurelia and Evangeline
x — Jennie Poh

A story for Every Season

The Fairy World

The Superfairies of Peaseblossom Woods use teamwork to rescue animals in trouble. They bring together their special superskills, petal power, and lots of love.

Superfairy Rose
can blow super healing fairy kisses to make the animals in Peaseblossom Woods feel better.

Superfairy Berry
can see for miles
around with her
super eyesight.

Superfairy Star
can create super dazzling
brightness in one dainty spin
to lighten up dark places.

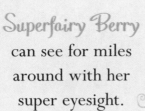

Superfairy Silk
spins super strong webs
for animal rescues.

Basil the Bear Cub

Table of Contents

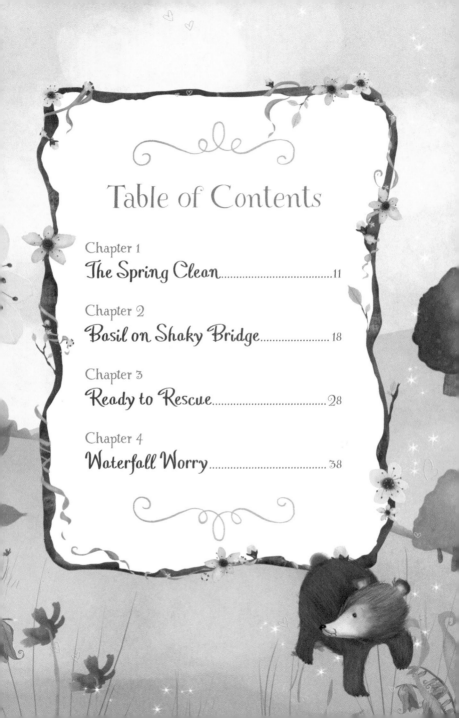

Chapter 1

The Spring Clean

The cold wind and snow of winter passed over Peaseblossom Woods, and the warm spring sun shone brightly over the trees.

Flowers bloomed.

Birds sang.

Bumblebees buzzed.

While the Superfairies were busy preparing for an exciting new season of animal rescues, all the animals of Peaseblossom Woods were slowly waking up from a long, cozy winter sleep . . .

"Yawn!" snuffled Susie Squirrel.

"Gosh, I'm so hungry!" squeaked Mrs. Mouse.

"Oh! What a lovely long sleep that was!" mumbled Mr. Badger.

"Splish-splash!" went Toby Otter as he flopped into the river.

"I'd like to explore!" said Basil Bear, rubbing his bleary eyes.

The Superfairies were busy spring cleaning their home inside the cherry blossom tree.

Rose was in charge of organizing their closet. She sang cheerfully as she washed all their pretty spring petal dresses and arranged their ribbons and dainty shoes.

"Roses and lilies, violets too. Blossom so pink, and bluebells so blue. Doo-be-doo-be-doo, flowers so true."

From time to time, she dreamed up some new dress designs, which she immediately doodled on her Strawberry computer.

"I'll show these sketches to the others later," she decided.

Meanwhile, Silk was dancing as she cleaned the bedroom and dusted the furniture with a feather duster . . .

twirl

hop

skip

spin
and repeat

She could hear Rose's song and soon joined in:

"Blossom so pink and bluebells so blue . . ."

Over in the storeroom, Berry was sorting through the supplies of honey, herbs, fruits, vegetables, and berries left over from the cold winter months.

She wrote labels for the jars and boxes:

Peaseblossom Healing Honey
Bumblicious!

Fresh Herbs
Peppermint. Parsley. Sage

Scrumptious Sweet Fruit
Tutti Frutti-tastic

Super Berries
Super Juicy. Super Yummy

Various Vegetables
for
Soups. Stews. Juice. and Dips

Berry began to hum along to the song as well:

"Doo-be-doo-be-doo, flowers so true . . ."

Meanwhile, Star was carefully counting and washing their collection of sparkling gemstones in a basin of spring water, lavender, and lemon juice. Sometimes they used the gems to help with their rescues.

"One moonstone. Twinkly.

Two rose quartz stones. Sparkly.

Three amber stones. Gleaming.

Four ruby stones. Dazzling.

Five sapphire stones. "Stunning . . ." she said to herself.

Then she caught a bar of the song, and joined in. *"Roses and lilies, violets too . . ."*

And the harder the Superfairies worked, the sweeter their song sounded. They loved to work as a team.

Chapter 2

Basil on Shaky Bridge

The sun grew warmer, and the day became brighter.

Down at the riverbank, Basil Bear Cub wandered along in search of a playmate.

He threw twigs into the water as he went.

"It's fun to be away from Mom and Dad!" he said. "But I'm a little bored on my own."

One of the twigs he threw made a huge splash!

The water splashed right over Toby Otter, who was lying on a big stone enjoying the warmth of the sun.

"Hey! What made that splash?" he cried, looking up to the riverbank.

"Oops, sorry — that was me!" called Basil. "I threw a stick. I didn't see you there."

Toby Otter sat up. "It's okay," he said. "Getting wet is what I do. Do you want to play?"

"Yes, please!" said Basil. "I'd love to!"

"Come down to the water," said the little otter.

Basil edged forward nervously.

"Come all the way down," said Toby Otter. "It's fun down here."

Back at the cherry blossom tree, the Superfairies had almost finished their cleaning work.

"It won't be long now until the animals wake from their winter sleep," said Rose as she hung up the last petal dress to dry. "It will be lovely to see them all again."

The Superfairies sat down to a delicious lunch together in their kitchen.

Berry brought a salad bowl from the storeroom, brimming with herbs, fruits, crunchy vegetables, and berries. Rose appeared with fresh lavender bread, which had come from the Badger's Bakehouse, spread with fresh butter from Fairydell Farm. All of this was washed down with minted peach-water.

"I can't wait to see our furry friends," said Rose.

"Me too!" chorused the other fairies.

"And there will be lots of new babies!" said Berry. "I love the babies!"

"Let's have some honeycomb and vanilla cake to celebrate spring," suggested Silk. She took a beautiful big cake tin down from the top shelf.

Then:

Ting-aling-aling . . .

There was a faint ringing sound in the distance.

"Does that sound like the rescue bells ringing?" said Berry.

"It does! It is!" said Silk. "One of the animals in the woods must be in trouble!"

Ting-aling-aling . . .

Ting-aling-aling . . .

The ringing got much louder.

"Oh, dear! We must get our wands as quickly as possible!" said Star.

"I'll check the fairycopter for fuel!" said Berry. "We'll definitely need the fairycopter if an animal has to be air-lifted to safety."

"Yes, and I'll grab our Strawberry computer!" called Rose.

"Let me fill the fairy rescue pack," said Silk.

In a twinkle-spin-flutter, the Superfairies were ready to rescue. They sat in their fairycopter, ready for take-off. Berry was at the controls as usual, because her super eyesight enabled her to see any problems ahead.

Rose checked the Strawberry computer to see where the problem was.

"Oh, look!" she said. "The screen on the Strawberry is showing a picture of Shaky Bridge — that's such a dark, dangerous spot!"

"Let's get going," said Berry. "Are we ready for takeoff?"

"I'll read through the checklist of what should be in our fairy rescue pack," said Star. "Let me know if you've packed everything, Silk."

☑ Extra Wings
☑ Warming Feather Cloak
☑ Peaseblossom Healing Honey
☑ Energizing Fruit Smoothie
☑ Healing Gemstones
☑ Olive Oil

"Nothing missing," confirmed Silk. "Ready for takeoff now."

"5, 4, 3, 2, 1 . . . go, go, go!" said Rose.

With the help of a passing gust of wind, Berry flew the fairycopter up, up, up over Peaseblossom Woods. Soon they were soaring in the sky. They followed the line of the river, swooping past Lavender Lane and the Strawberry Fields.

"It looks very dark up ahead at Shaky Bridge," said Berry, using her super eyesight. "Star, we will need all the brightness we can get. Please prepare to dazzle!"

"Ready to dazzle at any time!" said Star.

Chapter 3

Ready to Rescue

As they approached the part of the river where Shaky Bridge spanned the water, all the fairies except Berry flew out of the fairycopter.

Berry brought the fairycopter down, down, down . . . softly, gently, carefully . . . and landed it safely in a woodland clearing. Then she flew to join the others.

It was a very dark and gloomy part of the woods. The branches of the trees hung heavily over the river, and the wobbly old bridge cast looming shadows over the water.

Twinkle!

Dazzle!

Sparkle!

Tada!

"I will soon lighten this place up," said Star, using her powers of brightness. She began to spin.

The woods suddenly became bright.

"Thank you, Star," said Berry. "That's better. I can see clearly now."

"I can see Mother Bear by the bridge," said Berry, looking ahead. "She looks worried."

All the Superfairies followed Berry, and with their wands outstretched before them, they flew to where Mother Bear stood.

"Oh, thank you for coming," sobbed Mother Bear. "It's my new little cub, Basil. He wandered off and started playing with Toby Otter . . . and now he's dangling off Shaky Bridge! I think his paw is trapped!"

"Don't worry, Mother Bear," said Silk gently. "We will free him, you'll see!"

Toby Otter watched sadly from the edge of the water.

"I'm very sorry. I dared him to cross the bridge. It's all my fault!" he said. "I feel terrible."

"Well, I'm sure you won't do that again," said Rose. "You did the right thing by ringing the bell, Toby Otter!"

Father Bear stood in the water, talking up to his young son, who was hanging dangerously from the high bridge above.

"The Superfairies have arrived, Basil. Just do as they say, son," he said.

"Daddy, my paw hurts, and I'm very hungry!" said Basil.

Poor little Basil! He was so scared.

Rose flew in close to see what they could do.

"Hello, Basil," she said, blowing him a soothing fairy kiss. "Let me see what is trapping your paw."

"Your kiss has made my paw feel better," said Basil. "But it's still stuck."

The Superfairies fluttered around him, thinking about the best way to free him.

"A piece of wood is stuck across his paw. We need to remove it. Then he will be able to move," said Silk. The fairies worked very hard to move the piece of wood.

Star and Silk swished their wands over
it, hoping it might give a little, while Rose
and Berry tried to move the plank of
wood. But it was stuck firmly.

"I know what to do!" said Berry. "Let's pour olive oil over Basil's paw. Then we can slide it out from under the piece of wood!"

"Good thinking!" said Rose. "Take some oil from my backpack."

As soon as the oil was poured, Basil began to wiggle his toes to free his paw.

Wiggle. Wiggle. Wiggle.

Slip. Slide. Slither.

"My paw is moving. It's free!" he cried happily.

But it worked so quickly that Basil fell

into the river below!

Splash!

"Catch him, Father Bear!" cried Mother Bear.

Father Bear *tried* to catch him. Really he did. But Basil was carried along with the flow of the river.

"Help!" cried Basil. "I can't swim yet!"

"Superfairies! Please help. Quickly!" cried Mother Bear.

Basil ducked under the water. Toby Otter started to swim next to him, saying, "You can do it!"

Basil's eyes and ears were full of water, so he couldn't hear what Toby Otter was saying.

"I can't see!" he cried. "And I can't hear!"

And still the river's current pulled him along.

Chapter 4

Waterfall Worry

The fairies flew as fast as they could, following Basil, but after a group of rocks, the river was flowing in rushing circles of fierce water.

Basil was whirled and twirled around as if he was spinning inside a washing machine!

Whoosh! He went to the left.

Then whoosh! He went to the right!

Toby Otter couldn't fight the current either. He scrambled to safety at the water's edge, watching the rescue anxiously. "I wish I could do more to help!" he said.

"Berry, get the fairycopter!" said Rose. "And Star, take our speed wings out of the pack. Oh, and Silk, go with Berry and prepare a web ladder to throw down to Basil. Focus, everyone!"

The Superfairies stepped up their rescue operation, with Rose and Star hovering over Basil. It was impossible to reach him as he whipped around in the jets of bubbling water.

A strong current of water lifted Basil up and propelled him with a blast! back out into the fast-flowing open river.

Rose and Star followed him along the river, wearing their fastest wings.

Past Badger's Drift. Past Squirrel Square. Past Lavender Lane.

"Oh, no!" said Star. "Look! Basil is almost to the waterfall!"

"We *have* to save him!" said Rose.

"Basil!" called Star.

But Basil couldn't hear them because of the noise of the rushing water.

Berry and Silk flew overhead in the fairycopter and threw a web ladder down to Basil.

He didn't see it.

The waterfalls loomed up ahead. Rose knew it wouldn't be long before the little bear would be carried over the edge of the rugged rocks and thrown downwards, where the water poured like a faucet turned on full blast.

"Please do something!" said Mother Bear. "He will never survive the falls!"

Rose spotted the Duck Family nestling into the riverbank.

"Mr. Duck!" called Rose. "Can you paddle to Basil, please, and tell him there's a ladder coming his way!

"I'll do my best!" cried Mr. Duck.

Mr. Duck used all his strength to half-paddle, half-fly out toward Basil.

He got up close to him.

"Basil!" he cried. "Look up! The fairies will throw a ladder down to you!"

The poor little bear was exhausted, but with the last bit of energy in his body, he did as Mr. Duck said and looked up.

The ladder was dangling just above him.

At first, Basil didn't catch the ladder.
He tried again . . .

But it slipped through his tiny paws.

"You can do it, Basil!" called his father from the riverbank. "You're strong enough. I know you are! I believe in you! Try again!"

"Your daddy says you can do it!" said Mr. Duck. "Try again, Basil! You must!"

The brave little bear cub reached out for the ladder again. He used all his strength, and this time he grabbed it!

"Hooray! Don't let go, Basil," called Rose. "Good job! We're so proud of you!"

Basil was shivering and shaking and shuddering. The fairies flew around him and helped him to climb the web ladder, one rung at a time. He wobbled and swayed and sobbed.

"Another rung, Basil! You'll soon be at the fairycopter," said Star, "and we have some delicious snacks and juice in there!"

One rung at a time, he bravely wobbled his way to the top of the ladder.

At last, he was safely inside the fairycopter. Berry gave a thumbs-up to Mother and Father Bear below.

"Meet us back at the cherry blossom tree!" she called.

Mother and Father Bear set off as fast as their legs would take them.

"Bravo Basil!" said Rose. "You made it, little one!"

Basil's teeth chattered so much, he couldn't speak.

"Let's wrap him in the feather cloak," said Star.

Basil snuggled thankfully into the cozy cloak.

"I'm so, so, so, *so* hungry," he said in a croaky voice.

"How about some honey?" said Rose.

She offered him a spoonful of
Peaseblossom healing honey.

He licked the spoon. "I've never had
honey before," said Basil. "But I think I'm
going to like it!"

The fairies laughed and gave him some more, along with a tutti-frutti smoothie.

Berry landed the fairycopter back at the cherry blossom tree.

Mother and Father Bear were waiting.

Father Bear reached into the fairycopter and took Basil in his arms.

"Thank you, Superfairies!" said Father Bear. "What would we do without you?"

The fairies smiled proudly.

It was time for everyone to go inside the cherry blossom tree for some fairy fun!

The Bear family ate fairy cupcakes with the Superfairies and chatted until dark.

"From now on," said Basil, "I will never wander off without Mom and Dad again!"

Dancer the Wild Pony

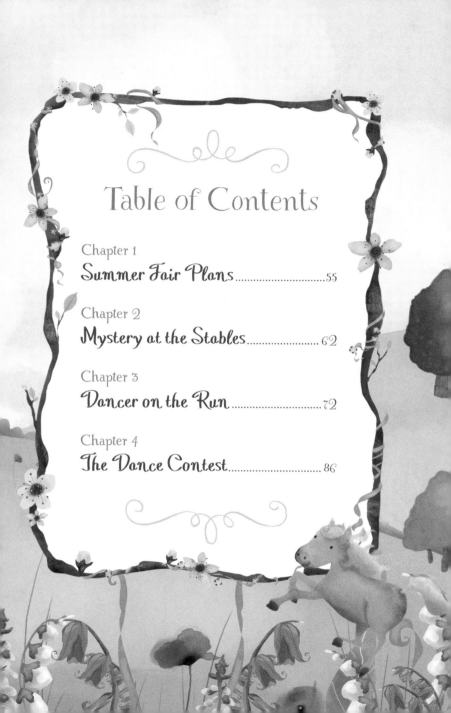

Table of Contents

Chapter 1

Summer Fair Plans

The sun was warm and bright, and the air was filled with the scent of roses and lavender. The river tinkled through Peaseblossom Woods, and the woodland animals relaxed in the soothing warmth of midsummer.

The Superfairies were very excited!

"Yippee! Today's the Summer Fair," said Rose. "It's always so much fun. I'm in charge of the contest to design the best fairy dress!"

"I can't wait. I'm going to sell superjams," said Berry. "I've been picking berries all week!"

"I'm going to help people make necklaces," said Star. She placed lots of sparkling gemstones in a box.

"The fair is always the best day of summer!" declared Rose. "I love seeing all the animals having fun."

"Let's decorate the cherry blossom tree with flowers and lanterns!" said Silk.

"Yes!" chorused the other three Superfairies.

"I *love* the dance contest at the fair!" said Star. "I so want to win this year!"

"Oh, Star. It's fun to take part, but you know Dancer the wild pony *always* wins," said Rose.

"Yes, she's a lovely dancer, the best in Peaseblossom Woods," said Star.

"But I won't give up hope," she added with a smile as she practiced her dance moves around the house.

The fairies started to decorate their house with branches of delicate blossoms and vases of pink roses. Then they heard the sound of bells ringing in the woods.

Ting-aling-aling . . .

Ting-aling-aling . . .

They all stopped what they were doing immediately.

"Listen! One of the animals needs us!" cried Rose.

She checked the Strawberry computer.

"What's the problem?" asked Berry.

"We've got to get over to Copperwood Stables as fast as possible!" Rose said.

"Oh, dear!" said Berry. "Can you see what's happening?"

"Yes!" cried Rose. "Dancer's in some kind of trouble. How terrible!"

"Dancer?" said Star. "Poor thing. I wonder what's going on. Let's get moving."

The fairies filled the tank of the fairycopter with spring water fuel from the pump, flew into their seats, checked their checklist, and were soon ready for takeoff.

There was no time to waste when a rescue was required.

"5, 4, 3, 2, 1 . . . go, go, go!" said Berry, at the controls.

The fairies were up in the air in the fairycopter in the swish of a flower wand.

"Perfect flying conditions," said Berry, at the controls. "Clear sky and no danger in sight. Hopefully this won't take long to figure out."

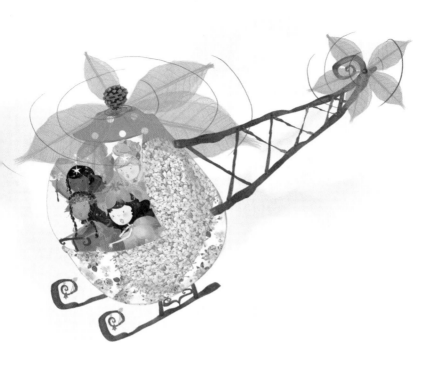

"I hope not," agreed Rose. "We need to get organized for the Summer Fair!"

The fairycopter fluttered over the leafy trees of Peaseblossom Woods.

Chapter 2

Mystery at the Stables

"There is Copperwood Stables down below," said Berry. She began to lower the fairycopter into a clearing in the woods. The fairies flew out of the fairycopter toward the stables.

Dancer's sister, Cloud, stood waiting for them at Copperwood Stables. She was alone.

"That's strange," said Rose. "Where's Dancer?"

The Superfairies all looked across the field for Dancer, but there was no sign of her.

"I'm so happy to see you," called Cloud as the fairycopter landed. "The thing is — Dancer has disappeared!"

"Disappeared? That's odd! Maybe she's just on an errand? When did you last see her?" asked Star.

"She was dancing away in the field, then I heard her sobbing. Loud, sad sobs. I came to find out what was wrong," said Cloud.

"Go on," urged Silk.

"I saw her cantering off toward the woods, throwing up dust behind her as she went," explained Cloud.

"How strange. She loves the dance contest at the Summer Fair," said Star. "I wonder why she was so upset."

"I don't understand what happened," said Cloud. "It's not like her at all."

"Can you think of anywhere she might have gone?" asked Rose.

"Well, she often has her hair decorated with flowers by the squirrels at their beauty parlor, so you could try there," suggested Cloud.

"Okay. Let's start at Squirrel Square," said Rose.

The fairies flew westward to where the squirrel family lived.

The squirrels were busy packing up their things for the Beauty Stall at the Summer Fair. They piled in strawberry shampoo, petal perfume, blueberry cream, and sandalwood soap. These were just some of the lovely things the squirrels made for everyone in Peaseblossom Woods.

Mrs. Squirrel came out to greet the Superfairies.

"Hello! I thought I heard the bells ring. How can I help you?" asked Mrs. Squirrel.

"Have you seen Dancer?" asked Silk.

"Not recently. We often put flowers in her mane, especially before dance contests. But not today, funnily enough," said Mrs. Squirrel. "Try the Frogs' house. She often chats with Mr. Frog."

"Will do, thanks Mrs. Squirrel!" said Silk.

The fairies flew immediately over to the riverbank and explained what had happened.

"Dancer's gone missing?" said Mr. Frog, with a look of shock. "That's very surprising!"

"She often likes to look at her reflection in the pond and chat with me about this and that," Mr. Frog continued, "but not today. Why not try the Mousey House? The mice said they had been talking to her about the dance contest."

At the Mousey House, Little Miss Mouse was busy fixing a bow in her hair.

"Hi, Superfairies!" she cried.

But she was soon very upset to hear about Dancer.

"Gone missing? Oh, no!" said Little Miss Mouse. "She was here yesterday. She said her dance wasn't good enough to win this year. I told her to practice and just do her best. I watched her dance and told her she did a lovely job, but she didn't sound as if she believed me."

The Superfairies began to get worried.

"Oh, how worrying," said Rose. "Can you think of *anywhere* else she may have gone to?"

"Hmmm, possibly to Badger's Dell. She likes to go there sometimes to see what Belinda Badger thinks of her dances," said Little Miss Mouse.

Over at Badger's Dell, the Superfairies saw dainty hoofprints in the ground.

"A clue at last!" said Silk.

"Let's follow the hoofprints!" said Berry.

The hoofprints were almost certainly Dancer's. They looked as if Dancer had been upset. The prints went this way, then that way, then around in circles.

Finally, the hoofprints stopped at the door of the Badger House.

Berry knocked on the door.

Chapter 3

Dancer on the Run

"Hello! Anybody home?" she called, peering in the window.

Mrs. Badger opened the door. "Yes?" she said rather sharply.

"Hello, have you seen Dancer?" asked Silk.

"Um, no, I haven't. Sorry, can't help you," said Mrs. Badger, slamming the door shut.

The Superfairies were suspicious. Mrs. Badger was usually so friendly.

There was a whinnying sound from inside the house.

"Her hoofprints stop here. I can hear her. She *has* to be in there," said Berry.

"But why is she hiding — and how do we get her out?" wondered Rose.

"I'll try to see what's going on inside the house," said Star. She peered in the little window. "I can't see a thing," she complained.

"Let me try," said Berry, squeezing in next to Star. "I *do* see Dancer! And Belinda too."

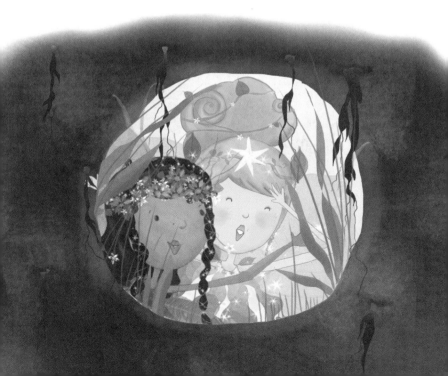

"What are they doing?" asked Rose curiously.

"Dancer looks very sad. Her head is low, and her eyes are glistening. She's been crying, I'd say," said Berry.

"If they won't let us in, we will have to get them out somehow," said Rose.

"Why don't I dazzle, and they'll all come outside to see what's going on," said Star.

"Good idea. It's worth a try," said Rose.

Star spun around, creating a big bright flash.

Twinkle. Sparkle. Dazzle. Ta-da!

The bright light dazzled in the dell. All the badgers came racing outside to see what was going on.

"We know she's in there," said Star. "Why won't she come out?"

"We can't tell you," said Mrs. Badger.

"You must! Cloud is worried and so are we," said Silk.

Mrs. Badger clearly wanted to help. She dropped her voice to a whisper. "She's worried about the dance contest — says she's forgotten how to dance. Got herself worked up, poor dear. Doesn't want to be in it this year, she says."

At that very moment, Dancer clip-clopped out of the house, heading toward the woods. She gathered speed and in a blink was racing into the distance. Powdery dust filled the air behind her.

"Dancer, come back!" called Silk. "Please! We can help you!"

But Dancer galloped wildly through the woods, while the Superfairies chased after her from the air above.

"Look out, Dancer!" cried Berry. "There's a huge hedge up ahead!"

Dancer cantered faster and faster. She jumped over the hedge . . . then landed safely on the other side . . . and carried on running.

She ran . . . and ran . . . and ran . . .

She came to Rabbit Ridge.

The rabbits were icing their huge carrot cake for the home-baking stall at the Summer Fair.

"Ah, that looks lovely!" said Mrs. Rabbit, wiping her brow as she stood back to admire her work. "I think that might be my best ever!"

Dancer galloped along so fast that she couldn't slow down.

"Dancer! Be careful!" cried Star. "You have to stop!"

Dancer was racing toward Mrs. Rabbit's carrot cake.

Her eyes were misty with tears, and she couldn't see well.

Mrs. Rabbit heard Dancer and turned around in time to see the sad little pony careering toward her — and her cake!

"Watch my cake!" cried Mrs. Rabbit.

Too late!

Dancer ran over the cake.

Squelch! Splodge! Splatter!

Dancer kept running.

Mrs. Rabbit looked up at the Superfairies. "You've got to stop her before she does any more damage!" she called. "I spent hours on this cake!"

The Superfairies could see that Dancer was going to run until she couldn't run any farther.

Dancer kept cantering. The Superfairies kept flying. Everyone was exhausted. But how could they get Dancer to stop?

Dancer came to a clearing that had five paths leading from it.

She seemed to hesitate for a brief moment.

"Perhaps she will stop here," said Rose.

Dancer decided to take the narrowest, trickiest path into the deepest part of the woods.

The Superfairies needed all their skills to follow her down the dark path and dodge between the branches.

Eventually, Dancer stumbled.

"What shall we do?" asked Star. "Her poor little legs!"

"Silk, you'll have to catch her gently in a web," called Rose. "We can't talk to her while she's out of control like this."

As Dancer stumbled along a narrow path between the trees, Silk dropped a web in front of her.

Dancer couldn't go to the left . . . and she couldn't go to the right.

She came to a stop as the web folded around her.

"Leave me alone!" she cried. "I don't want to go to the stupid Summer Fair!"

"We want to help because we care about you!" said Rose, blowing a healing kiss.

"I'm no good at dancing now!" Dancer cried. "Please don't make me dance!"

Rose's kiss landed on Dancer's pretty nose. She settled down after that.

"Come on, Dancer. You're the greatest dancer in Peaseblossom Woods. We *need* you at the Summer Fair!" said Star.

"I can't do it!" sobbed Dancer. "It's horrible when everyone *expects* you to be the best every year. I am so nervous!"

"Oh, you poor thing," said Rose. "Why don't you dance with Star this year?"

Dancer's face broke into a sweet little smile.

"I suppose I could try that," agreed Dancer. "It would be lovely to dance with her — if she wants to."

"I'd love to!" said Star. "It would be an honor."

Dancer giggled. "This could be fun!" she said.

Rose was relieved — she had been so worried that Dancer would get hurt. But she was safe and well. And with any luck, she would still be in the dance contest.

Chapter 4

The Dance Contest

Before the Summer Fair, Star and Dancer had a picnic lunch by the cherry blossom tree.

"What should we do for our dance?" asked Star.

"I've been practicing something special," said Dancer. "Do you want to see?"

"Yes, let's go further along the riverbank and try out some moves," suggested Star.

"That's great," said Dancer. "After that, would you like to come with me to have flowers put in our hair?"

"Oooh, I'd love that," said Star.

Dancer and Star had their hair done with matching pink flowers.

Everyone in Peaseblossom Woods was happy and calm as the Summer Fair began. All of the animals arrived with baskets and food and decorations and balloons. The young animals enjoyed playing games. The moms and dads chatted and ate cupcakes. Mr. Otter took barge trips along the river.

At last, it was time for the dance contest.

A huge audience gathered to see Star and Dancer dance together.

They danced a scene from *Cinderella*.

Mr. Badger played on an old piano.

Dancer and Star made dainty jumps, spins and hops.

It was the prettiest dance anyone had ever seen.

"Well done!" said Rose. "That was truly lovely."

Dancer was so nervous when it was time for the winner to be announced that all the fairies hovered around her to make sure she didn't run off again.

"And the winner is . . ." announced Mr Mouse. "Ah, we have two winners this year — Star and Dancer!"

A huge cheer went up in the crowd.

"Best dance ever," said someone.

"A lovely partnership!" said another.

"How sweet," said Little Miss Mouse.

"Hey, we both won this year!" laughed Star as they received floral garlands from Mr. Mouse.

The four Superfairies lay back on the grass with the sun shining on them.

Dancer turned to all the Superfairies. "Thank you for giving me back my confidence," she said. "I'm sorry I've tired everyone out!

"Phew, we are tired," said Rose. "But it's time for our song!"

The Superfairies formed a fairy circle, while Dancer danced in the middle. The fairies sang their rescue song.

Dancer danced merrily along the riverbank.

"Hey, come back!" called Rose.

Dancer cantered straight back. And she promised not to run away the next time she felt nervous!

Martha the Little Mouse

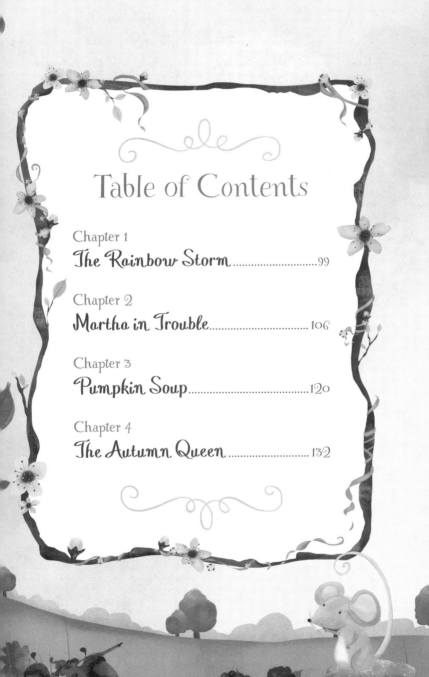

Table of Contents

Chapter 1

The Rainbow Storm

Superfairy Rose was busy in the cherry blossom tree making a skirt from golden autumn leaves.

Meanwhile, out in the woods, Martha the Little Mouse and Susie Squirrel held hands and danced around in circles under the big oak tree. It had been raining heavily all morning, and now a huge rainbow was in the sky.

"It's quite sunny now. Shall we go off on an adventure?" suggested Martha.

"I'm not sure," said Susie Squirrel. "Mom and Dad said there's going to be an autumn storm later."

"How could there be a storm when the sun is shining?" giggled Martha. "Grown-ups exaggerate. Let's explore!"

The girls set off along the woodland floor, looking for somewhere to play.

They heard familiar voices. "That's Basil the Bear Cub and my brother Sidney!" said Susie. "Let's see what they're up to!"

The girls teamed up with the boys and chased each other through the woods.

"Autumn is so pretty!" said Martha. "I love the golden leaves and all the berries and fruits!"

But before long, raindrops fell through the copper-colored trees.

Plink! Splash! Splatter!

The rain got heavier very quickly. It spilled onto the carpet of leaves as if a faucet had been turned on.

Crackle! Splish! Splosh!

A cold wind whipped angrily through the woods.

Whoosh! Swish! Flap!

The sky became very dark.

"What happened to the sun?" said Martha.

"It looks like the sky is frowning!" cried Basil Bear.

Martha looked up. "Oh, look! It's the Autumn Queen flying over the woods!"

"Yes," said Sidney. "She's bringing a big storm with her!"

"Oh, she's beautiful!" gasped Martha. "But I'm scared. Why does she have to bring such an angry storm every autumn?"

"Because she needs to shake off all the leaves for winter!" explained Basil.

"The trees have to sleep while we do. And while they're sleeping, the new buds of spring start to grow. They couldn't be green all year — they would run out of energy. That's what my Dad told me. And he knows everything."

"I wish it could just be summer all year!" said Martha. "I love sunshine."

"That would be boring," said Basil. "I love storms! This is exciting!"

"I don't like it. I'm going home now," said Martha. "I want to be safe and cozy with Mom and Dad."

All the young animals began to scuttle back to their families for shelter and food.

"See you later, Martha," called Susie, as she went off in the opposite direction of her best friend.

Chapter 2

Martha in Trouble

That night, as the Superfairies snuggled into their cozy beds in the cherry blossom tree, the wild storm raged around them.

"Oh, I hate storms!" said Rose as the wind howled and whistled, making the whole blossom tree sway in the wind.

"It should be over by morning," said Star.

"Goodnight, everyone!" called Silk.

"Goodnight!" said all the Superfairies.

But —

Ting-aling-aling . . .
Ting-aling-aling . . .

"Oh, the animals need us!" cried Rose. "I will have to be brave for them."

Rose took courage from the other fairies. They wrapped up warmly in their autumn cloaks. Then they flew out through the wind and rain to the fairycopter. They climbed inside.

"Rose, what does the Strawberry computer show?" asked Star.

"It's the poor little mice!" said Rose. She examined her computer screen. "The wind has blown the roof off the Mousey House. They're freezing!"

"Hurry up. We can bring the mice back to the cherry blossom tree in the fairycopter and make them cozy here for the night!" suggested Silk.

"Yes, we have plenty of space for them. We'll give them pumpkin soup and hot chocolate and iced gingerbread," said Rose.

"This could be a bumpy ride," said Berry as she started up the fairycopter.

The other three Superfairies held hands.

"Ready for takeoff!" announced Berry. "5, 4, 3, 2, 1 . . . go, go, go!"

Berry used her super eyesight to steer the fairycopter safely through the storm, but it was choppy.

The fairycopter fluttered to the east . . . and to the west . . . to the north . . . and to the south. But Berry managed to steer back on course, using the big gusts of wind to power them.

They soon landed in front of the Mousey House with a tremble, a bump, and a thud!

The whole Mouse family was huddled together in a corner of the roofless house.

"Thank goodness you've arrived!" said Mr. Mouse.

Little Martha was delighted to see the Superfairies. She ran toward the fairycopter excitedly.

"No, Martha! The wind's too strong. Stay in here," called her mother.

But Martha was already out on the woodland floor.

"Thanks for coming, Superfairies!" said Martha. "I hate storms!"

But with that — whoooossssh! A gust of wind whisked the dainty mouse into the air and twirled her around wildly between the branches.

"Oh, my baby!" cried Mr. Mouse.

They all watched helplessly as Martha
began to . . .

spin

twist

tumble

and twirl

She flapped around the treetops with
the autumn leaves circling her.

"Superfairies to the rescue!" cried Rose,
finding her own courage at last. She flew
from the fairycopter out into the windy
woods.

The fairies held hands and fought against the wind as they fluttered toward Martha.

But as they got close to her, a fresh blast of wind swirled the feather-light little mouse off in the opposite direction.

"Help me!" cried Martha, as she was whisked out of reach.

"We'll save you!" called Silk.

Martha was carried in the air through the woods. As the Superfairies and Mouse family followed her, the other animals in the woods became concerned too.

The Squirrel family watched Martha twirl over the treetops. They were so worried that they got too close to the edge of their nest. It tipped up, falling down from their tree! Down the squirrels fell with it.

Bump! The nest and squirrels landed on the woodland floor.

All the squirrels were a bit shaken up by the fall.

"Are you all right?" called Rose.

"Yes, we're fine," said Mr. Squirrel.

However, Susie Squirrel, who was best friends with Martha, got very upset indeed to see her friend twirling about the treetops. She began to sob.

"I will climb to the top of the tallest tree and try to reach over to Martha!" she said.

"No!" cried Berry. "It's too dangerous! Stay with your parents, Susie!"

But the little squirrel set off regardless, longing to feel useful.

She scurried to the top of a huge oak tree and held onto a curving branch. She leaned out over the wood, stretching as far as she could toward her best friend.

The Superfairies hovered between Martha and Susie.

Susie was determined to take hold of her friend.

"Take my hand, Martha," she called as the little mouse continued to flap around the sky between the trees. "Pleeeeeease."

Martha tried to reach Susie.

Their arms were outstretched toward each other.

They nearly touched.

Almost. But not quite.

The Superfairies gathered round Martha, trying to scoop her in their arms.

"I'm so tired!" called Martha.

"We're doing all we can," said Rose. She blew healing kisses at the little mouse.

There was a brief break in the gusts of wind, so Martha dropped down below the treetops, where it was more sheltered.

The Superfairies managed to gather around Martha now.

"Stay in close to her," advised Star.

The fairies guided Martha toward the branch Susie was on.

"Come on, Martha, you can do it," said Susie. "You'll soon be safe and cozy if you just reach over to me."

With Susie's sweet voice in Martha's ears and the Superfairies guiding her, she finally made it to the branch of the tree!

Chapter 3

Pumpkin Soup

"Hold on, Martha," cried Star.

"Hooray!" cried all the animals on the woodland floor below.

The Mouse family danced around in a circle.

"Wait on this branch," said Berry, "and I will go and get the fairycopter. Then you girls can hop in."

"Yay, we get to go for a ride in the fairycopter!" said Susie, hugging her friend excitedly.

They wobbled on the branch.

"Whoa!" said Susie. "We don't want to fall off, do we?"

"Exactly," said Rose, "so be very still and careful until Berry arrives!"

Silk called to the animals below. "Everyone, make your way to our cherry blossom tree, but hold hands as you go. And be very careful of the wind! Just go in and put some logs on the fire!"

The Superfairies helped Martha and Susie into the fairycopter. Then Berry flew everyone safely back to the cherry blossom tree.

"Phew! I'm exhausted!" said Berry as she landed the fairycopter. "That was quite a rescue!"

"I know," agreed Rose. "Wasn't Susie wonderful? Let's heat some soup, warm some bread, and sit around the fire, shall we?"

"Yes," agreed Berry. "That sounds lovely."

The rest of the mice and squirrels were already in the sitting room, toasting their toes.

The Superfairies got busy warming up pumpkin soup, icing gingerbread, whisking hot chocolate, and toasting marshmallows.

The strong winds raged around the tree house.

Once everyone was served, Rose sat very quietly, listening for the bells, just in case.

She looked deep in thought.

"What are you thinking about?" asked Silk.

"About how much harm this storm is causing," said Rose. "And what we can do about it."

The Superfairies invited the animals to stay overnight with them. "Make yourselves at home," said Star.

Meanwhile, Rose called a meeting of the Superfairies.

"What's wrong?" asked Berry as they gathered around the kitchen table.

"I think we should all go to see the Autumn Queen now," said Rose.

"Why?" asked Berry.

"Yes, what for?" wondered Star.

"We need to tell her that this storm is hurting the animals. She will understand," said Rose.

The Superfairies decided there was no time to waste.

"Shall we wear our formal cloaks?" asked Berry.

"Of course," said Rose. "We must show our respect to the great queen. We should not anger her in any way."

Rose continued. "We need to find her kindness. It colors the woods with gold and bronze and copper. It ripens the harvest so we can eat in the winter. I know it's there."

The Superfairies tucked the animals into bed with hot chocolate.

"We have some work to do," explained Rose. "But you rest well, and let us hope the woods are calmer by morning."

"Goodnight — and thank you!" said Mrs. Mouse. She held Martha close to her as they snuggled up for the night in one of the Superfairies' spare flower beds.

The fairies then brushed each other's hair until it was smooth and shiny. They dressed for their important visit to the Autumn Queen's Corner.

Rose wore a silver cloak and her silver crown.

Star wore a golden cloak and her golden crown.

Silk wore a lilac cloak and her lilac crown.

Berry wore a ruby red cloak and her ruby red crown.

Rose led the way as they held hands and flitter-fluttered through the swaying trees in search of the powerful Autumn Queen.

The leaves from the beautiful trees of Peaseblossom Woods floated around them like golden confetti.

The fierce winds were not calming, and the rains still fell. Rose knew they were doing the right thing. If only they could find the beautiful Autumn Queen, Rose felt sure they could ask her to calm the storm.

"This looks familiar!" said Star as they arrived at an enchanting corner of the woods. They entered a pathway leading to the secret fairy throne room.

Gold and silver tree branches arched over the pathway. It was perfectly calm and sheltered. There were glowing lanterns hanging in the branches that lit the way to the throne room.

"I always forget how beautiful it is!" whispered Berry.

They arrived at the entrance and looked in.

A vast throne of twisted twigs and bronze leaves sat in the middle of the room.

But the Autumn Queen was not on her throne.

"Where is she?" whispered Berry.

"She will appear," said Rose. "I know it."

Nothing happened. The fairies hovered.

"She cannot be rushed," said Silk. "She's super busy as it is her own season."

Rose nodded.

After a few moments, the Superfairies heard a rustling of leaves.

They blinked, and the beautiful Autumn Queen magically appeared on her throne!

Chapter 4

The Autumn Queen

She was majestic. Her long hair gleamed, and her golden gown sparkled. A crown of branches framed her pretty face. The Superfairies bowed before her.

Rose moved a little closer to the queen.

"We are sorry to trouble you," said Rose.

"I know why you've come, and I'm sorry about the storm," said the Autumn Queen. "But it's my job to make the trees ready for their winter sleep. I send the winds to bring down the leaves, and sometimes they get rather wild."

"Yes, of course," said Rose. "But the animals are suffering."

"I send the rain to make sure there is plenty of water to drink in winter," the queen explained. "I try my best to think of what the animals will need in the cold months."

She added, "But I don't want to cause suffering. I love the animals as you do."

"We know that," said Berry, stepping forward. "But we had to rescue Martha today after the wind picked her up. We very nearly lost her."

"Oh, that's terrible," said the queen. "Let me work some magic . . ."

"Thank you," said the Superfairies.

"You do very important work here in the woods," said the queen, "and we are all grateful for it."

"It is our pleasure," said Silk. "We work with the seasons, not against them."

The Autumn Queen smiled kindly, then nodded her head to show the Superfairies that they should leave.

They flew back a different way. They followed the lines of the river, listening to owls hooting as they went.

By the time they got back to the cherry blossom tree, the storm was starting to calm.

"Ssssh," said Rose. "The animals will be sleeping."

The Superfairies crept into the house.

"Surprise!" cried Martha and Susie. "We couldn't sleep so we thought we'd have an autumn party!"

"Oh, how lovely," said Rose.

The Superfairies giggled.

"Great surprise," said Berry. "Is that the pumpkin soup I smell?"

"Yes!" said Susie. "And more iced gingerbread!"

Rose went to lock the big door. She looked outside. The night sky twinkled with bright stars.

"Hey, everyone," she called. "Looks like the storm has passed over."

"Hooray!" said Martha, dancing. "No more winds!"

"Let's gather around the fire now," said Rose, "and sing songs! It's time to celebrate autumn!"

Violet the Velvet Rabbit

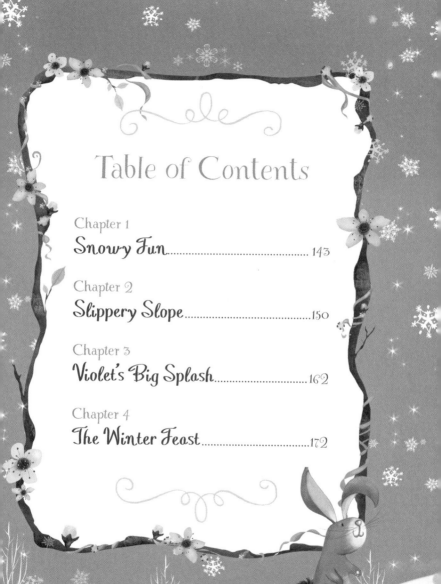

Table of Contents

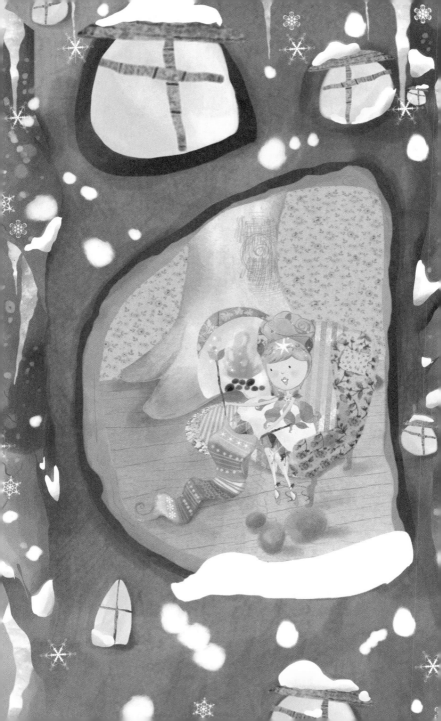

Chapter 1

Snowy Fun

A flurry of soft snow fell over Peaseblossom Woods. It covered the landscape like powdered sugar on a cake.

It was certainly a cold winter.

Glassy icicles dangled from bare branches. Twinkly snowflakes clung to bony twigs. The air was scented by winter berries and spices.

The Superfairies of the cherry blossom tree knew the woodland animals would be cold and hungry.

At this time of year, they took extra super care of their animal friends.

Inside the Superfairies' cherry blossom tree home, everything was very cozy. A log fire crackled and lanterns glowed. A freshly baked batch of golden honey bread rested on a rack.

Superfairy Star busily knitted hats and scarves for all the young rabbits and squirrels.

The other Superfairies planned the very last feast of the year for all the animals. It would take place in the cherry blossom tree.

Rose read from a menu she had been working on for days. "How does this sound?" she asked.

"Mmmm. Lovely! And let's toast marshmallows on the fire afterwards! And have dancing too!" said Star, who loved to dance.

Lentil & Cinnamon Soup

Honey Bread with Cheese

Mushroom & Walnut Risotto

Sweet Potato Bake

***

Lavender Meringues

Almond Iced Star Biscuits

Orange Drizzle Cake

Chocolate Peppermint Creams

"Yes," agreed Silk. "And we'll light candles and hang garlands of holly!"

"Oooh, it's going to be wonderful this year," said Berry. "Let's get to work."

Out in the woods, it snowed steadily until there was more snow than any of the young animals had ever seen before.

Despite the biting cold wind and their rumbling tummies, the little creatures of Peaseblossom Woods thought that playing in the snow was great fun!

Sam Squirrel skated on the frozen lake. Wheeeee! Bump! It was very slippery! Sam fell over. But up he got!

Martha Mouse caught the falling snow. "Snowflakes are so pretty! I wonder if they really are all different?"

Billy Badger and Basil the Bear Cub
threw snowballs . . . of course! "Haha, you
miss me every time, Billy!" teased Basil.

Farrah the Fawn made patterns in the
snow with her feet.

Violet the Velvet Rabbit and Susie Squirrel made skis from wood. Oops, Susie took a tumble! The ground was very uneven under the pretty snow.

Dancer and Cloud, the wild pony sisters, pulled a sled through the woods.

"Will you join us?" they called out to
all the little animals. "We are searching for
gifts for the Superfairies as a way of saying
thank you for all they do!"

"Coming!" called the young animals.

"The Superfairies are so kind. Let's find
them beautiful gifts!" said Violet.

"Yes, what would we do without them?"
said Susie.

Chapter 2

Slippery Slope

The young animals all set off to gather gifts with the ponies.

"There are always lovely pine cones as well as pretty snowdrop flowers at the bottom of Snowdrop Slope," said Violet the Velvet Rabbit. "Why don't we go there first?"

"Do you know how to get there?" asked Cloud.

"Oh, yes!" said Violet. "I've been there lots of times!"

All the animals followed Violet.

However, things looked a little different when covered by deep snow, and the blizzard was still blowing.

"This way!" called Violet. She waved everyone through the woods, though she did not feel at all confident.

When they came to a crossroads in the woods, Violet was very confused.

"Well," said Farrah, "which way do we go? You said you knew the way!"

"I thought I did," said Violet. "But I'm not completely sure now . . ."

"Oh, dear!" said Martha Mouse. "Does this mean we're lost?"

"We just need to look for the big slope," said Violet. "That's what I normally do."

"But we can't see past our noses," said Susie, "because of all this falling snow."

Susie looked down the possible paths.

Orlando the Owl flew to the top of the trees.

"I think I can see Snowdrop Slope this way," he said.

They all followed his lead.

But Orlando was better at seeing in
the dark of night than on a snowy day.
After a while, he flew onto a branch, quite
exhausted.

"You don't know where we are, do you, Orlando?" said Susie, looking up at him.

"I'm afraid I don't," admitted Orlando.

Violet twitched her nose. She thought she could smell snowdrop flowers.

"I think I know which way to go!" she said. "Everybody, follow me!"

But the animals were nervous about following Violet, because she'd gotten lost before.

"Please!" said Violet. "Trust me. This time, I really do know where I'm going, I promise!"

"Come on, everyone!" said Susie. "Anyone can get lost once. I believe Violet will find Snowdrop Slope!"

There was a lot of mumbling, but finally everyone agreed to let Violet lead the way.

Violet followed her nose through a dark section of the woods.

"We're almost there," she said.

Once they got through the woods, there was the slope!

"Ta-da!" said Violet proudly.

At the bottom of the steep slope, they began to collect pine cones for the Superfairies. But Basil found that a bit boring.

"Let's slide down the slope!" he suggested to the others. "I dare you!"

Some of the animals were too scared.

"I'm in lots of trouble already for getting carried away by the wind in autumn," said Martha. "I had better not do anything silly."

"Scaredy!" said Basil. "Violet, are you too frightened as well?"

"No!" said Violet boldly. "I'll do it! Nothing scares me."

"Are you sure about this?" asked Martha. "Wouldn't you prefer to stay and just watch Basil whizz down?"

"No, he's not the only brave one around here," said Violet. "I'll take my skis. Wish me luck!"

Martha looked worried. "Good luck, Violet. You're so brave," she said.

So Basil and Violet climbed their way to the top of Snowdrop Slope.

"Oh, no!" said Violet as she looked down the slope. "What a long way down!"

"I'm not even going to think about it!" said Basil. "You follow me down. Wait until a few minutes after I've left. See you at the bottom!"

"Could we hold hands and go down together?" asked Violet.

"No, we might bump into each other," said Basil. "And anyway, you have the skis. Don't give up now, Violet. You are so cool for coming up here. You can do it!"

Basil launched himself fearlessly down the hill.

Glee!

Sheeee!

Whoosh!

"This is so much fun!" called Basil. "I've never gone so fast!"

"I'm going to try it now!" announced Violet bravely, getting her skis into position.

"Don't do it!" called Martha.

"Crawl down carefully!" cried Susie.

For a few moments, it looked like Violet was undecided, but then she made up her mind to . . . goooooooooo!

"Aaargh!" she cried, as she slipped down the slope, falling on her bottom. Her skis and poles went flying in the air.

Violet raced down as fast as a snowball.

"Help!" she cried. "I don't like this! Help me!"

Oh, no! The slope was so slippery, she went faster and faster.

At last, she came to a sudden stop at a sharp ledge of snow. She hung on to the ledge, dangling over a deep valley below.

"Rescue me!" she cried. "Somebody, please! My paws are so cold . . . I can't hold on here for much longer."

Chapter 3

Violet's Big Splash

The log fire danced merrily in the fireplace of the Superfairies' sitting room. The woolly hats were all knitted, while the toasty winter feast was ready at last!

Ting-aling-aling . . .

Ting-aling-aling . . .

The warning bells began to tinkle.

"Oh, dear! The animals need us!" said Star. "I was so afraid something might happen in this dreadful weather."

"I couldn't bear for anyone to be hurt," said Rose. "Superfairies! Action!"

The Superfairies pulled their fluffy winter wraps around them and put on their floral boots. They picked up the warming feather cloak and flew out to the fairycopter.

Rose quickly checked the Strawberry computer.

"What can you see?" asked Silk.

"It's showing Violet the Velvet Rabbit hanging on to a ledge of snow! She must be freezing!" said Rose.

"I can hardly see with the falling snow. I'll do my best. 5, 4, 3, 2, 1 ... go, go, go!" said Berry.

The fairycopter lifted up into the snowy winter sky.

When they landed at Snowdrop Slope, the little animals were huddled together, fretting about Violet the Velvet Rabbit.

The Superfairies looked up to the ledge where Violet was in peril.

"Wait there," called Rose looking up to the top of the slope. "We're on our way!"

"Thank you!" called the Velvet Rabbit. "I'm really scared! And my paws are about to let go!"

The Superfairies set off to get her.

But Violet's voice rolling down the hill seemed to have made the snow under her rumble.

There was some rippling movement in the snow, and a low, thundery sound grumbled in the air.

A great mass of snow began to roll downhill. The tiny rabbit was caught up in the middle of it. She tumbled down the slope, carried along by the fast-moving snow.

"Help me!" she cried, her voice muffled by the rush of snow around her. "I can't stop!"

The Superfairies flew above her, following the little Velvet Rabbit's speedy progress down the slippery slope.

Rose tried to stop the snowball with a healing kiss, but the kiss missed. The snowball was going too fast!

Silk dropped a ladder, but Violet could not grab it.

Star and Berry were able to get closer to Violet, but she was covered in too much snow for them to grab her.

At the base of the slope, Violet bumped against a tree trunk lying flat along the ground, and was promptly thrown high into the air, flying in a curve.

Where would she land?

The Superfairies followed her anxiously.

All the young animals ran toward her as she started to drop down. She was getting lower . . .

and lower . . .

and lower . . .

Smack! Crack! She landed on the middle of a frozen pond.

The Superfairies dashed to the scene while the animals waited at the water's edge.

"Stay still, Violet!" called Silk from above. "The ice is very thin . . ."

"It's not that thin," said Violet, feeling excited about being so close to safety. "I can make it to land!"

"Please don't move!" called Rose.

But Violet was too excited and began to bunny-hop across the pond.

Bounce,

bounce,

bounce,

crack!

Oh, no!

The ice around Violet broke up and —

$\mathcal{S}$plash! She fell into the freezing pond below!

"$\mathcal{A}$aargh!" cried Violet. "It's so cold! It's horrible! I want Mommy and Daddy!"

Above Violet, the Superfairies got into a huddle to plan how to help her.

The little bunny bobbed around in a dark, watery hole in the ice.

Chapter 4

The Winter Feast

Star dazzled the water with brightness so they could see her clearly.

Twinkle. Sparkle. Dazzle. Ta-da!

"That's better!" said Silk.

"Now go in for her!" said Rose.

Silk and Berry swooped in toward Violet at top speed, while Star hovered as back-up.

They reached down for her, plucking her freezing little body from the icy pond in one move.

The Superfairies' arms didn't look strong enough to carry the little rabbit across the pond. But luckily the Superfairies are super strong.

"Hooray!" cried all the animals, as the Superfairies wrapped a shivering Violet in the warming feather cloak.

Rose blew lots of healing kisses.

Violet gave a great shudder. Then a huge shiver. Followed by a little giggle.

"I think I'm going to be fine!" she said.

The Superfairies smiled with relief, but they had to talk to Violet about what she had done.

"You know it was very silly to go to the top of the slope," said Berry.

"I'm sorry," said Violet. She didn't want to tell the Superfairies that Basil had encouraged her.

However, Basil felt guilty. "It was my fault," he blurted out. "I said Violet would be a scaredy if she didn't come up to the top!"

Rose looked very disappointed, which made Basil feel terrible.

"Violet could have been very seriously hurt," said Rose. "And so could you. This could have spoiled the whole Winter Feast."

"I know," said Basil. "I won't do anything like that again! I promise."

"Make sure you don't," said Rose. "Let's forget it for now, but be more careful in future."

The Superfairies flew Violet in the fairycopter back to the cherry blossom tree for the Winter Feast.

The other animals arrived on the sled, pulled by Dancer and Cloud, with the older family members following on.

"Let's decorate the cherry blossom tree now for the Superfairies!" said Cloud.

"Oh, thank you," said Rose.

The animals strung garlands of berries and pine cones across the tree house. They placed holly and ivy along the fireplaces and left gifts of nuts and dried fruits.

The woodland friends ate the delicious Winter Feast given by the Superfairies and sang songs around the toasty log fire.

After that, the animals snuggled up together for a big sleepover.

The next day, the animals had to go
back to their own homes for the long
winter sleep.

"Bye, Superfairies. Thanks for
everything!" called the animals.

The Superfairies gathered around the fire,
nibbling on tasty leftovers from the feast.

"Phew, it's been quite a day," said Star.

"Quite a year, actually!" agreed Berry. "Our rescue skills have been well tested."

"At least the animals can't get into trouble when they're asleep!" said Silk.

"That's true," said Rose. "But we will miss them so much!"

"Yes, but before we know it, spring will be here!" said Star. "We can look forward to that!"

"Yes," said Rose. "But until then, let's stay cozy together!"

"Why don't we dance to celebrate a good year of rescues!" said Star.

The other Superfairies giggled. Star liked to dance whenever she could!

The Superfairies held hands and danced inside the cherry blossom tree.

Fairies from the blossom tree,
Superskills galore have we.

Caring in this charming wood
For needy animals, as we should.

Twinkle, sparkle, dazzle, swish,
Tending animals as they wish.

And when a rescue's nicely done,
It's time to have some fairy fun.

Dancing, singing, twirling, glee,
All around our blossom tree!

Which Superfairy Are You?

1. If you had an allowance, you would . . .
   A) save it up for an adventure
   B) buy jewelry
   C) buy books
   D) buy hair clips and accessories

2. When a friend is sad, you . . .
   A) take her out for an ice cream
   B) listen to the problem
   C) do a favor to make life easier for her
   D) play music and dance

3. If asked to clean your room, you would start by . . .
   A) putting away the clothes and shoes
   B) putting away the jewelery and bags
   C) putting away the books
   D) putting away the dress up stuff

4. You prefer perfumes that smell like . . .
   A) lavender
   B) rose petals
   C) fruits
   D) honeysuckle

5. If your grandma wasn't feeling well, you would . . .
   A) talk to her about when she was young
   B) give her flowers
   C) bake a strawberry cream cake
   D) perform a dance routine for her

6. Which herb or spice smells nicest?
   A) lavender
   B) cinnamon
   C) nutmeg
   D) mint

7. What is the best way to travel?
   A) airplane
   B) bicycle
   C) helicopter
   D) train

8. Which insect do you like most?
   A) silkworm
   B) butterfly
   C) ladybug
   D) bumblebee

Mostly A —You are like Silk. Adventurous and brave, you always think of ways to deal with problems! You enjoy action and adventures.

Mostly B —You are like Rose: gentle, kind, and loving. You are good at staying calm and love pink things.

Mostly C —You are like Berry: fun, always helpful, with lots of great ideas. You are sensible and wise.

Mostly D —You are like Star. You cheer people up and dazzle with your sparkling ways! You are funny and enjoy jokes and dancing.

Superfairies
Sugar Cookies

It's not a party in Peaseblossom Woods without fairy food! Celebrate the seasons like the Superfairies and their friends with scrumptious sugar cookies. Sprinkled with pixie dust, these edible fairy wings are the perfect treat to serve at your next fairy tea party!

What You Need

- ♥ 1 tube of premade cookie dough, sugar-cookie flavor
- ♥ Frosting in your favorite colors (fairies prefer green, pink, white, and purple)
- ♥ Sugar sprinkles
- ♥ Butterfly-shaped cookie cutter
- ♥ Rolling pin
- ♥ Baking sheet

What To Do:

1. Ask a grownup to help you roll out the cookie dough into a ½-inch-thick circle. Use your cookie cutter to cut out cookies in the shape of fairy wings.

2. Bake the cookies as directed, making sure to keep an eye on them so they don't get too crispy! (Don't forget to have a grownup help you when you're using the oven.)

3. Let the cookies cool completely. Once they're ready, decorate each one with frosting. Then add sugar sprinkles.

4. Enjoy alone or serve to guests at your fairy tea party!

All About Fairies

The legend of fairies is as old as time. Fairy tales tell stories of fairy magic. According to legend, fairies are so small and delicate and fly so fast, that they might actually be all around us, but just very hard to see. Fairies, supposedly, only reveal themselves to believers.

Fairies often dance in circles at sunrise and sunset. They love to play in woodlands among wildflowers. If you sing gently to them, they may appear.

Here are some of the world's most famous fairies:

The Flower Fairies

Artist Cicely Mary Barker painted a range of pretty flower fairies and published eight volumes of flower fairy art from 1923. The link between fairies and flowers is very strong.

The Tooth Fairy

She visits us during the night to leave a coin when we lose our baby teeth. Although it is very hard to catch sight of her, children are always happy when she visits.

Fake Fairies

In 1917, cousins Elsie Wright and Frances Griffiths said they photographed fairies in their garden. They later admitted that most were fakes — but Frances claimed that one was genuine.

About the Author

Janey Louise Jones has been a published author for ten years. Her Princess Poppy series is an international bestselling brand, with books translated into ten languages, including Hebrew and Mandarin. Janey is a graduate of Edinburgh University and lives in Edinburgh, Scotland, with her three sons. She loves fairies, princesses, beaches, and woodlands.

About the Illustrator

Jennie Poh was born in England and grew up in Malaysia (in the jungle). At the age of ten she moved back to England and trained as a ballet dancer. She studied fine art at Surrey Institute of Art & Design as well as fashion illustration at Central Saint Martins. Jennie loves the countryside, animals, tea, and reading. She lives in Woking, England, with her husband and two wonderful daughters.